W9-BKU-111

When the Parkway Came

When the Parkway Came

Anne Mitchell Whisnant & David E. Whisnant

PRIMARY SOURCE PUBLISHERS Chapel Hill, North Carolina

© Copyright 2010

Anne Mitchell Whisnant and David E. Whisnant

All rights reserved

Designed by Richard Hendel

Manufactured by Regent Publishing Services,

Hong Kong,

Printed April 2010 in ShenZhen, China

10 9 8 7 6 5 4 3 2

To our sons

Evan and Derek

and

to all the parents and children

who travel the

Blue Ridge Parkway

Acknowledgments

Writing and illustrating this book has been a wonderful new challenge, and we are very grateful to many people who have helped in the process.

Centrally important to the project are the images we have chosen to illustrate the story. Longtime Parkway photographer Mike Booher of Asheville, N.C. generously allowed us to search his personal archive for Parkway images, as did local collector John Nunn of Galax, Virginia. Blue Ridge Parkway archivist Jackie Holt has responded effectively and expeditiously to our numerous requests, as have the University of North Carolina at Asheville Special Collections librarians Helen Wykle and Sallie Klipp. The Digital Library at Virginia Tech supplied a number of images, and their staff (especially Jane Wills) were unfailingly helpful. Rhonda Broom of the Norfolk Southern Corporation (successor to Norfolk and Western) allowed us free use of two images we had been unable to find elsewhere. The North Carolina Collection at the University of North Carolina at Chapel Hill supplied several other images. Michael Southern, Senior Architectural Historian and GIS Coordinator for North Carolina's Historic Preservation Office, located rare photos of the Glendale Springs Inn. Librarians at the public library of Galax, Virginia provided helpful direction at an early stage. Both Kevin P. Schlesier, Exhibits and Outreach Librarian at North Carolina State University, and Kim Andersen Cumber, Archivist at the North Carolina State Archives, helped us to find a surprisingly elusive photograph of R. Getty Browning.

It was not all about illustrations, however. Anne's long time friends and colleagues Marla Miller and Alexandra Lord read the manuscript meticulously; their excellent suggestions have improved it greatly.

David's daughters Beverly and Rebecca read the manuscript and offered helpful advice, as did Anne's parents Norma and Joe Mitchell. Our sons Evan and Derek accompanied us on countless drives up and down the Parkway and gave us suggestions on the text from a young reader's standpoint.

Finally, we are enormously grateful to our good friend and colleague Rich Hendel, for many years responsible for all book design at the University of North Carolina Press. Rich was perhaps the earliest person to suggest that we should undertake this project. He followed through with excellent advice at every stage, and ultimately designed the book for us. How you see it here owes much to his vision and skill.

Our hope is that this book will delight and inform young readers and enrich their experience of the Blue Ridge Parkway. They are its future. For now, we also hope that the book will encourage their parents to view supporting the Parkway — indeed our entire national parks system — as an important part of their role as citizens, and as parents.

When the Parkway Came

The year I turned eight, my Mom was working weekends, and Dad was building a room onto our house. So my granddaddy Jess Miller – Papa Jess, I called him – kept me every Saturday for months.

Lots of times, especially after the leaves began to turn, Papa Jess liked to take me out for rides in his old '65 Mustang. One day, right after lunch, we started up our usual route – Highway 321 out of Lenoir toward the mountains. Most of the time, I enjoyed the curves and twists. It was like a roller coaster. But that day, between the big lunch, the musty hot smell of the vinyl back seats, and the swaying and dipping of the car, I felt a little queasy. Finally we got to the ridge, turned, and the road flattened out. We were on the Blue Ridge Parkway again – Papa Jess's favorite drive of all.

I loved those trips up on the Parkway. "I love them so much," I told him this time, "that I don't even mind your old Mustang." Sometimes Papa Jess and I took a little fish net and went on a hike down to Crabtree Falls, or stopped to see our favorite rocks in the Minerals Museum.

Other times we walked under the huge Linn Cove Viaduct. "Did you ever see boulders this big?," Papa Jess asked me one day as we climbed over one after the other. And of course I hadn't – not by a long shot.

But today we just drove on awhile. I had almost fallen asleep when the breeze stopped blowing in. Papa Jess had pulled off the road. "Wake up, Ginny."

Beyond a fence by the side of the road, a beautiful meadow stretched out. I didn't recognize the place. "Where are we, Papa Jess?"

"Come on." He climbed the fence and lifted me over.

We threaded our way through the tall grass till we came to a big rock. I climbed up and sat down. "See that spot over there," he asked, "where that little rise is? That's where it was."

"Where what was, Papa Jess?"

"Our house. And we had a barn that was up on that curve right over there – a little to the right of the one that's there now. Our road came in just beyond that." His blue eyes got a little glassy, and he began to tell me a story I'd never heard before – about himself when he was my age, and his Mom and Dad and sister Maggie, and about how the Parkway came and took part of their farm.

"I remember it was late in the summer," he said. "Daddy had come in out of the field and was reading the paper while Mama was doing some mending. Daddy was never much good at relaxing, but he did try to keep up with the news."

Our farm had 70 acres, and it took all the hard work both of them could do to keep the place going. The house wasn't big, and our barn was sort of ramshackledy, but every time we came up the road home, we thought it was the most beautiful place anybody could ever live. And best of all, Daddy had built us a big pond behind the house.

We didn't have much money, but we had everything we needed – cows and chickens and pigs and apple trees and a big garden my mama and daddy planted every year. So we had plenty of vegetables and canned applesauce, bacon and ham from the hogs, all the milk we could drink, and butter for Mama's hot biscuits.

In the last few months, though, things had gotten really hard. It was right in the middle of what they called the Depression. Us kids didn't really know what that meant, except that nobody, including us, had much money. People that had gone off to find jobs in the milltowns down the mountain were drifting back, saying the mills had closed and there weren't any jobs anymore.

And it seemed like every day somebody else's farm was put up for sale.

The E. P. Simms Farm Now Owned By W. A. Clarke, Sells

At Public AUCTION

Friday, September 27, 1935

10:30 A. M.

On The Premises, Near Elk Creek, Virginia

Description and Location

On State and National highway 21, about two miles South of Elk Creek High School, on the waters of Elk Creek, Subdivided into different tracts, about 90 acres, you can buy as much or as little as you want: 30 acres of good nice bottom land, a very productive farm: good dwelling house, two good barns and other out-buildings, running water to the house. Rural route passes by the house.

No better tract of land for sale in Grayson County. Title absolutely good, no lien against this property.

TERMS: 20% Cash, Balance in One, Two and Three Years' Time

Music By The Famous Buck Mountain Band

Free Lunch - - - - Sacks of Sugar to the Lucky Guessers

Personal Property

HORSES,   TRUCKS,   FARM MACHINERY

Don't Forget The Time—On Lucky Friday, September 27, 1935.

Being Sold by the Request of the Owner

PARSONS AUCTION COMPANY

"Sellers Of The Earth"   Independence, Va.

Through it all, Mama and Daddy kept talking about President Roosevelt and how he was going to help us.

They said the government was giving people jobs building dams over in Tennessee, and schoolhouses and parks and such all over the country.

I was lying on the floor playing with some little toy cars when Mama nudged Daddy's foot. "The paper says they're gonna build a road through here, Gene."

"'Bout time," Daddy murmured, half asleep.

"Some kind of 'Parkway' they're callin' it," she said. "Gonna run from that new park in the Great Smokies to the other new one in the Shenandoah Valley – over 400 miles long they say it'll be. Sounds like it might be something like that big new road they opened over at Fancy Gap a few years ago."

Mama read on, "Says here them business men down in Asheville had a lot to do with it."

We had never even been to Asheville. But the paper said Asheville was in a real bad way. In the 20s, they'd done an awful lot of building down there – lots of new neighborhoods, big old tall government buildings, and fancy hotels.

And then the Depression hit, and the tourists – who didn't have any money either – stopped coming. The Asheville hotel men thought the Parkway would bring the tourists – and their money – back, so they worked hard to make sure it would pass close to town on its way to the Great Smokies.

While Daddy dozed, Mama turned the page. "Gene, it says they'll be hiring men to work on it. They're startin' construction next week up at Low Gap."

Daddy sat up and took the paper from Mama. "I don't know," he said. "Probably be a lot of men lined up there to try to get work. But I reckon I'd have as good a chance as anybody."

"And you can do anything, Gene," Mama said. "Ain't never been nothin' needin' doin' on this farm you couldn't do, one way or another."

"I got nothin to lose," Daddy said. "Might as well give it a try." The next Wednesday morning he woke Maggie and me up earlier than usual. Mama had us a good breakfast ready, and some stuff packed to eat on the road.

About daylight, we all climbed in the truck and started up towards Galax. "Some men down at the store said a train is coming into Galax today with some bulldozers and trucks for the Parkway work," Daddy said as we pulled out of the driveway. "I think there may be a big new steam shovel, too."

"There's the river!" Maggie shouted when we got close to town. "I can see the railroad running beside it, and yonder's that big old steel bridge."

We crossed the bridge a while before we got to town, and turned down Main Street. On the way to the depot we passed a house way bigger than ours on the corner of Virginia Street, and then the Bluemont Hotel – the biggest building I had ever seen. "Wish we could stay there," Mama said. "Maybe someday, but not now, for sure."

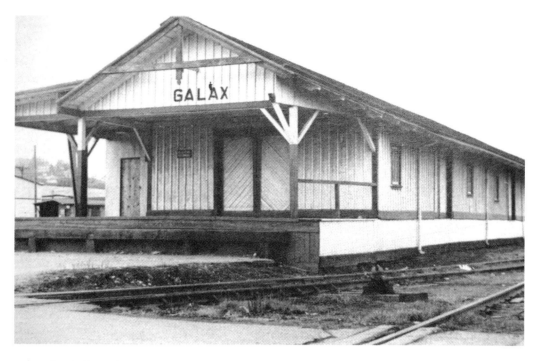

A whole lot of men were gathered around the station, but the train wasn't there yet, so Maggie and I looked for something to do, thinking maybe we should have stayed at home.

"Come on, Jess," Mama said, "let's you and Maggie and me walk down to Globman's store. Somebody told me Mrs. Globman went all the way to New York city to bring back the new fall fashions." Mama knew we didn't have money to buy anything, but she liked to look, anyway. The walk was more fun for Maggie and Mama than for me, but I was glad to go along to pass the time.

14

When we got back, we watched some men unloading lumber from another train, but before long we heard the train whistle, long and low, but getting higher as it came nearer.

Pretty soon the train pulled in, stopped, and let the air out of its brakes with a big "Whooosssshhh."

"Look way back toward the end of the train," I called to Maggie. "There's the steam shovel." That's what we called it before we learned that it was really a diesel shovel.

It was a whole lot bigger than I expected. Behind that was another car with two bulldozers, and behind that were some other cars with big dump trucks on them.

For the next hour or two, we watched men climb onto the train, crank up the trucks and machines, and drive them down the ramps they had pulled up to the cars. Then they loaded some of the machinery back on the trucks to take it to where they planned to start building the road.

Finally Maggie and I saw our chance, and we ran and climbed up into the steam shovel. "What do you think this lever does, Jess," Maggie asked as she tried to yank on it. "Beats me," I said, standing on two pedals that were way bigger than my feet. Right then we heard Daddy calling. "Jess, Maggie, get on back in the truck. We got to go down to Glendale Springs for a little while."

Glendale Springs wasn't too far from our farm. There was a boarding house there – an "inn" they called it – that some fancy lawyer in town owned. "They're hirin' men to work," Daddy said, "and they said the foreman's stayin' over at the inn. They need some more help next week, and they said if I get over there today, I might could sign on."

So we took off down the road, and after while we pulled up in front of the inn. There were lots of men milling around outside. "Sure looks like a lot of people need work," I said to Daddy. "Yeah," he said a little sadly, "and I'm one of 'em."

Maggie and I waited in the truck while Daddy went around to the back door and inside. Pretty soon, he and another man came out and shook hands. We could see Daddy smiling as he walked back to the truck.

"Your Daddy's going to start helpin' to build that parkway next week," he almost sang, and that "happy days are here again" song we'd heard on our Philco radio flitted through my head.

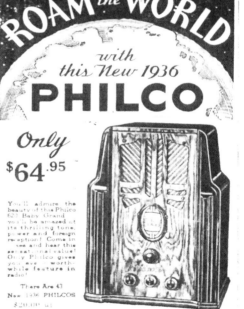

Maggie and I perked up. "I hope this means you'll be driving the steam shovel," she told Daddy. On the way home, we asked him a lot of questions. "Where will you be working, Daddy? What will you be doin'? Will it be dangerous? What's that road gonna be for, anyway? How close is it going to be to our house?"

"I don't know much about it yet," Daddy said. "All I know is that I have to be up at Low Gap early Monday morning to help clear some land."

Once he started working, though, he came home every day and told us what he saw. "There's bulldozers and trucks and big shovels everywhere," he said. "You'd never believe how much dirt and rock they're moving."

After Daddy had been working a few weeks, Maggie and I came home from school one day to see a new black Buick parked in front of the house and our old dog Bruno barking and pacing in the yard. We knew that if Mama saw us she'd send us back out to get the mail and put out a salt block for the cows, so we snuck up under the kitchen window to listen. "Here, stand on my shoulders," I told Maggie, "and see if you can hear what they're saying." I lifted her up so she would be just high enough, but not so high they'd see her.

Mama and Daddy were talking to a man we'd never seen. "Mr. Browning," they called him.

Mr. Browning had spread out some maps on our kitchen table, and he and Daddy were standing over them. "It'll come along right about here," Mr. Browning pointed out. "I've walked over the whole route," he told Daddy. "It's going to be a beautiful park and road for everyone. You'll be able to see forever from right here on your ridge. It'll be like driving in the clouds."

Mr. Browning sounded so excited as he told stories about bear hunting, hiking, snakes, great high waterfalls, and a trip to the west he'd taken with his family on a road called Going-to-the-Sun. He said they had just finished building it, and our parkway was going to be something like it.

We could have listened to him all afternoon, but before long Mama came out and called us. We scurried around and tried to look like we were just coming up the road, but she wasn't fooled. "Jess and Maggie," she called, "get on out there and get the mail and put out that salt block I told you to put out this morning." Bruno loped along behind us, looking hungry.

By the time we did all the chores and got back inside, Mr. Browning was gone.

At supper time I could tell Daddy was really worried. "That Parkway is going to come right through the middle of our farm," he blurted out, "and I ain't got any idea how much land they're gonna take."

"But it'll be fun to see the bulldozers and steam shovels," Maggie and I said, almost at the same time. Daddy and Mama just looked down at their plates. We didn't understand why.

A few days later when we were at Mr. Penland's store, Mr. Penland said that Mr. Browning had put up some maps on the courthouse wall in West Jefferson. We stood on the steps outside the store and talked with some neighbor men a few minutes, but then Daddy said, "Come on, kids, we're goin' to the courthouse to see what this is all about."

When we got to West Jefferson, Daddy took one quick look at the maps and got white as a sheet. "Twenty acres? That's almost a third of our whole farm," he said. "And we ain't even gonna be able to get to that new road to drive on it, 'cause they won't allow us to cut no driveway to it from what farm we're gonna have left."

Somehow, even after he'd been working on the Parkway several weeks now, and even after Mr. Browning had visited, Daddy really hadn't understood. "Ain't never heard of a road like this before. Roads is supposed to be for people that lives on them to *use*, but this road ain't like that. And that ain't right," he almost whispered. We drove home not saying anything to each other.

Mama and Daddy sat in the living room talking for a long time that night, and Maggie and I listened through our open bedroom doors.

Their chairs squeaked as they fretted over their account book. "Only $5.50 an acre – that's a hundred and ten dollars for the whole thing, plus that's some of our best land," Daddy said. "We won't have enough left to keep the farm going. How'll we make it?" "Yeah," Mama said, "and I heard they paid bigger prices than that for some of Judge Clarkson's land down at Little Switzerland."

"You know what else?" Mama said, "Somebody at church told me that a lawyer up in town is helping people get better prices for their land from the government." "We ain't got money for no lawyer," Daddy sighed. "We ain't even gonna have money to buy gas for the tractor and the truck."

Ohids, N.C.
Jan. 7, 1937.

Mr Franklin D Roosevelt.
My dear Sir

I am writing you in regard to my farm, on the Blue Ridge mountain, where the Park to Park high way goes. It goes through the middle of my farm, the right of way takes 20 acres out of the middle of my farm. I just have 70 acres of land in all, just leaves me a small piece of land on each side. The state dont offer me the worth of my land, not counting the damages any thing—

...ruined my ... and take all of ... They just offered ... dollars and said ... ld not give any ... land is good ... better than ... the Blue Ridge ... that they have ... prices for ... ud is for government ... it looks like ... afford to pay a ... ice for it. ... dont have enough land left to make my support. I would like to sell it all to the government. I dont want no great big

price for my land. I just want a reasonable price just what it cost me, would satisfy me. I dont believe the government would take less than ... I always supported the ... ratic party and ... act too. and I ... they ought to ... when I need help. ... some people would ... the land on the ... e isn't any ... ll we people have ... support on it and ... good to us ... Park to Park high—

The next night Daddy sat up late at the table in the living room, a small lamp shining on one of our school tablets. He was writing to the president.

My dear Mr. Roosevelt:

I am writing you in regard to my farm on the Blue Ridge Mountain where the Park to Park highway goes. The right of way takes 20 acres out of the middle of my farm. I just have 70 acres of land in all. Just leaves me a small piece of land on each side. The state don't offer me the worth of my land. Maybe some people would say that the land on the Blue Ridge isn't any good. Well we people have made our support on it and it is some good to us and the Park to Park highway isn't any benefit to us according to what they tell us. We aren't allowed to put any buildings near it and not even cross it to our land on the other side. Will you please write me and tell me if I am wrong and what for me to do.

Daddy always voted Democratic, and we listened to President Roosevelt on the radio. "I'm just sure the President will help us get a fair price for the land. At least what we paid for it," he said. "Maybe the Parkway people could just buy up the whole farm, and we could move down to Asheville or somewhere where I'd have some chance to get a better job."

By Saturday of that week, Maggie and I were kind of beginning to understand what some of this might mean. We just wanted to get off by ourselves and think about it, so we took Bruno out and walked all over the farm.

We loved the animals, the spring house and smoke house, Mama and Daddy's huge flower and vegetable garden, the barn Daddy had built, and the pond behind the house. We had a nearly new tractor, and after they had had a good crop year, Daddy had put a Delco lighting system in the house.

Sitting under the big tree by the creek with Bruno sleeping beside us, we talked about how Mama and Daddy had poured themselves into this place for nearly twenty years. "I feel sad for them," Maggie said. "Yeah," I said, "and for us, too."

"It ain't fair," Maggie said. "They ain't got no right to take our place. 'Specially not for all them rich people to come drivin' in here just to see the scenery."

But I remembered Mr. Browning and his hikes and his Going-to-the-Sun road, and I thought about this new road in the clouds and about all the people that would get to see our beautiful mountains. "I feel sort of confused about it," I told Maggie.

For the time being, anyway, all we could do was wait.

Daddy went to work every day that fall while Mama and Maggie and I kept the farm going. Carving through our mountains took big machines and explosives, and he was driving the big dump trucks and learning how to do some surveying.

Daddy seemed to feel a little bit better as the paychecks kept coming in, and he was proud of the road they were building, even if some of it was dangerous work.

Sometimes on Sundays we'd get in the truck and go to see the big arched stone bridges they were building. "I've never seen bridges like these," I said. "I can't wait till we can drive over or under them." Daddy knew some of the men who were building them, and sometimes they would let us get out and walk across.

Before long, though, the surveyors came to our place. They tramped through the corn, waded through the spring, and put out little stakes where the Parkway would go.

We moved the fields and fenced a new pasture, and with the money Daddy was making on the Parkway, everything seemed to go OK for a while. Maggie and I were kind of excited to see the construction on our place actually begin.

Finally, a check for our twenty acres arrived in the mail. It was for $600.00 – a lot more than we had expected, but still not much for what all we had to give up. For that little bit of money, they cut the middle right out of our farm. And of course it wasn't just our farm – some of our neighbors were talking about what was happening to them too.

Maggie cried the day they tore down the barn; I cried, too, but I didn't let anybody see me. Daddy said he couldn't stand to watch, so he went off to work while the construction crew at our place toppled it over and trucked the wood away.

Before long they opened a section of the Parkway near us. As soon as Daddy got a day off, he and Mama packed us a picnic lunch and piled us all in the truck to go take a look.

Hard as it had been for us, it *was* like Mr. Browning had said. We were driving in the clouds. "I've never seen the mountains look like this," I told Mama.

We pulled over at a few spots where they had cut out the trees so you could see the blue hills rippling out like the sea. I looked out and felt my chest swell like the waves.

Maggie and I counted the license plates on the other cars – Georgia, Virginia, North and South Carolina, even as far off as Pennsylvania.

After we drove on for a while, we turned off at a place they called Cumberland Knob, where government workers were building a big shelter. Some kids at school had talked about going up there. We grabbed the lunch and a tablecloth and scrambled up the short hiking trail to a picnic place they had already built back under the trees.

After lunch we rambled over the trails while Mama and Daddy talked to the Caudills, our neighbors from up the road. They said they'd been coming to Cumberland Knob every weekend since it opened.

Back home, we kept the farm going, but barely. Daddy didn't have time to build a new barn, and our best field was gone. When the big war came, he volunteered to go, and we took him to the train. Watching him leave was even sadder than watching our barn being torn down.

After Daddy left, Mama had Maggie and me to help. We were bigger then, and could work harder, but it wasn't enough, especially since we weren't getting his checks for working on the Parkway.

When Daddy came home after the war, he and Mama talked about what to do. "It's hard to think of leaving the farm," I heard him tell her. "Yeah," she sighed, "especially if we have to move somewhere where we don't know nobody, or have family or friends to help each other like people always does around here." "I know," Daddy said, "but the furniture plants in Lenoir are

paying good money, and I hear there's plenty of jobs." After many nights of talking like that, they decided to sell what was left of the farm and move down off the mountain.

Long after he got a furniture plant job, Daddy would come home in the afternoon and tell Mama he wanted to move back to the mountains. But we never did.

One day we heard that the Parkway bought up the rest of the farm and tore down the house and everything else.

It had been a long story, and I had been sitting on that big rock by the Mustang for a long time. Papa Jess took his handkerchief out of his pocket and wiped his eyes. "I'm glad we had our farm while we had it," he said, "and that my daddy – all of us, really – had a part in building this road through our mountains. I wish he could have seen it all finished; he would have been so proud."

"I wish this land was still ours, Papa Jess," I said. Papa Jess was quiet for a while. Then he looked up and smiled. "It is, Ginny," he said. "It still is. Yours, mine, and everybody's. And it is still so beautiful."

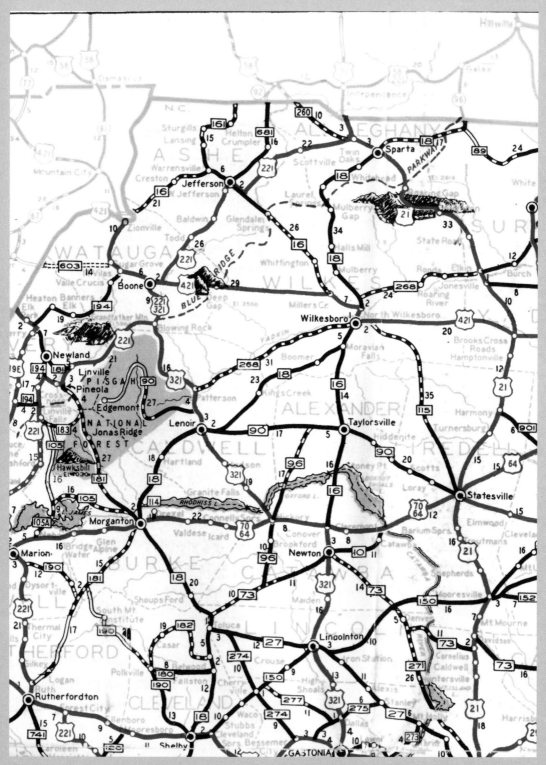

State Highway System of North Carolina, 1936

The Parkway's Past and Future A Historical Note

The Blue Ridge Parkway is a 469-mile scenic road winding through the beautiful southern Appalachian mountains. Set within a narrow corridor of protected land, it is – as its name suggests – a "way through a park." The Parkway joins two of the great eastern National Parks, Shenandoah in Virginia and Great Smoky Mountains in North Carolina and Tennessee. Since the late 1940s, it has been the most visited site in the entire National Park system.

In recent years, more than eighteen million visitors have traveled parts of the Parkway every year. They drive to places where they can pull off the road to see a distant view, enjoy spring wildflowers or colorful fall leaves, get out for a short hike, or set up a tent at a campground.

How does it happen that we have this wonderful Parkway? During the Great Depression of the 1930s, millions of people lost their jobs. To give them useful work, President Franklin D. Roosevelt created a set of programs called the "New Deal." People employed by New Deal programs built schools, dams, roads, hospitals, parks, and swimming pools, and worked on many other worthwhile projects all over America.

The Parkway was one of those projects. Business leaders – especially around the city of Asheville in North Carolina – promoted it because they hoped it would bring tourists to spend money in hotels, restaurants and shops. Politicians hoped construction would provide jobs for local citizens.

Parkway engineers and designers, especially North Carolina highway engineer R. Getty Browning, laid out a route that would let people see glorious mountain views, secluded coves, and dramatic waterfalls. Construction of the Parkway began in the fall of 1935. The last stretch, the "missing link" around

Grandfather Mountain, North Carolina, was finally completed more than fifty years later, in 1987.

People from everywhere love the Blue Ridge Parkway. We are all fortunate to be able to enjoy it. But many people don't know that creating it required sacrifices that have now mostly been forgotten.

The states of Virginia and North Carolina used a government power called "eminent domain" to buy over 40,000 acres of private land for the Parkway. Some of it was land that farm families had long lived on and loved. Most of them had no choice about whether to sell. Sometimes they weren't paid much, and sometimes they did not see how the Parkway would benefit them. Some of them resented how it disrupted their lives, and wondered why some other owners got better deals for their lands.

This book tells the story of one of those families. Though some particulars of the family's story are fictional, many of the events and situations are true. The family is based on the life of S. A. Miller, who owned a small farm straddling the Wilkes and Ashe County lines in the vicinity of Parkway milepost 263, just east of West Jefferson, North Carolina. In late 1935, the State of North Carolina took about twenty acres of Miller's farm for the Parkway. Having initially been offered only $5.50 an acre for what he knew was good farmland, Miller wrote a letter to President Roosevelt complaining that the price was too low, and that the Parkway "isn't any benefit to us." His letter is preserved at the National Archives in Washington, DC. Other historical documents show that the state eventually paid Mr. Miller $600 for his land.

Mr. Miller's story reminds us that when we create something beautiful for everyone, some people may have to give up something they cherish. As citizens, we must understand how this grand project came to be. We must not forget the work of so many hands, and the sacrifices some people made. And we must preserve and protect our Parkway for generations to come.

Image Credits

Title page. Blue Ridge Parkway color photograph. Photo by Mike Booher.

Title page. Boy and his dog, Mitchell or Yancey County, North Carolina, ca. 1934. Photo by Bayard Wootten, North Carolina Collection, University of North Carolina at Chapel Hill.

Page 1. Entering Blue Ridge Parkway. Photo by Mike Booher.

Page 2. Crabtree Falls, Blue Ridge Parkway. Photo by Mike Booher.

Page 2. Rocks and minerals. Photos by Evan Whisnant.

Page 3. Linn Cove Viaduct, Blue Ridge Parkway, fall 2008. Photo by David Whisnant.

Page 4. Blue Ridge Parkway with barn in fall. Courtesy Blowing Rock Historical Society.

Page 5. Rebecca Whisnant on Blue Ridge Parkway, ca. 1977. Photo by David Whisnant.

Page 5. Boy and his dog, Mitchell or Yancey County, North Carolina, ca. 1934. Photo by Bayard Wootten, North Carolina Collection, University of North Carolina at Chapel Hill.

Page 6. Living Room of Paul Erickson, farmer, 1940. Farm Security Administration - Office of War Information Photograph Collection, Library of Congress.

Page 7. Farm with pond, near Blue Ridge Parkway. National Park Service Digital Image Archives.

Page 7. Mr. and Mrs. Fred Hornshell in food cellar, Black Lick, Virginia. Virginia Cooperative Extension AGR 2455, Special Collections, Digital Library and Archives, University Libraries, Virginia Polytechnic Institute and State University.

Page 8. Operator of thread making machine, Laurel cotton mill, Laurel, Mississippi, 1939. Southwest Virginia: Maps and Posters MAPS0006, Special Collections, Digital Library and Archives, University Libraries, Virginia Polytechnic Institute and State University.

Page 8. Simms farm sale announcement. Grayson-Carroll (VA) *Gazette*, 19 September 1935.

Page 9. Franklin D. Roosevelt in car waving hat, 1938. Courtesy Franklin D. Roosevelt Library.

Page 10. Asheville *Citizen* headline announcing Parkway route. Asheville *Citizen*, 11 November 1934.

Page 10. Fancy Gap road opening announcement, 1928. Southwest Virginia: Maps and Posters MAPS0006, Special Collections, Digital Library and Archives, University Libraries, Virginia Polytechnic Institute and State University.

Page 11. Pack Square, Asheville, 1920s. E. M. Ball Collection #1896, D. H. Ramsey Library Special Collections, UNC Asheville 28804.

Page 12. Unemployed workers in line. Courtesy Franklin D. Roosevelt Library.

Page 13. Carrico Bridge, Galax, Virginia. Courtesy John Nunn, Galax, Virginia.

Page 13. Main St. looking south, Galax, Virginia. Courtesy John Nunn, Galax, Virginia.

Support and Advocate for Your Parkway

Blue Ridge Parkway Foundation (http://brpfoundation.org/):
The primary fundraising organization for the Parkway. Sponsors the North Carolina Blue Ridge Parkway license plates, which raise money for Parkway enhancements.

Conservation Trust for North Carolina (http://www.ctnc.org):
Raises funds to protect Parkway vistas in North Carolina.

Eastern National (http://www.eparks.com/store/):
A Parkway cooperating association that sells educational items at all visitor centers, returning a percentage of the sales to the park.

Friends of the Blue Ridge Parkway (http://www.blueridgefriends.org/):
A membership organization that mobilizes volunteers who assist with Parkway projects.

National Parks Conservation Association (http://www.npca.org/):
Advocacy organization dedicated to protecting and enhancing all of the national parks.

Western Virginia Land Trust (http://www.westernvirginialandtrust.org/):
Raises funds to protect Parkway vistas in Virginia.

Learn More about the Parkway and the National Parks

Blue Ridge Parkway homepage (http://www.nps.gov/blri)

Blue Ridge Parkway Association (http://www.blueridgeparkway.org/):
A non-profit organization of businesses serving visitors in the Parkway region.

Blue Ridge Parkway Blog (http://www.blueridgeparkwayblog.com/):
Group blog exploring history and current issues.

National Park Service History website (http://www.nps.gov/history/history/index.htm):
Contains extensive historical information about the National Park Service and its parks.

National Park Service History and Culture website (http://www.nps.gov/history/index.htm):
Contains extensive information about the parks, arranged by historical and cultural topics.

National Parks Traveler (http://nationalparkstraveler.com/):
Wide-ranging commentary on history and current challenges facing all of the national parks.

Anne Mitchell Whisnant, author of *Super-Scenic Motorway: A Blue Ridge Parkway History* (University of North Carolina Press 2006; http://superscenic.com), writes and speaks widely about the Parkway and the national parks. She is an administrator in the Office of Faculty Governance and an adjunct faculty member in the Department of History at the University of North Carolina at Chapel Hill. In a thirty-five year career at several universities, **David E. Whisnant** taught and wrote widely on Appalachian history and culture. His books include *Modernizing the Mountaineer: People, Power, and Planning in Appalachia* (rev. ed., University of Tennessee Press, 1994), *All That Is Native and Fine: The Politics of Culture in an American Region* (University of North Carolina Press, 1983), and *Rascally Signs in Sacred Places: The Politics of Culture in Nicaragua* (University of North Carolina Press, 1995). Anne and David are co-founders of Primary Source History Services (http://prisource.com), through which they do research and write for the National Park Service. They live in Chapel Hill, North Carolina with their sons Evan and Derek.